The
DISAPPEARING
Fruit

AN INTERACTIVE MYSTERY ADVENTURE

by Steve Brezenoff
illustrated by Marcos Calo

Field Trip Mysteries Adventures
are published by Stone Arch Books
a Capstone Imprint
1710 Roe Crest Drive
North Mankato, Minnesota 55603
www.mycapstone.com

Library of Congress Cataloging-in-Publication Data
Names: Brezenoff, Steven, author. | Calo, Marcos, illustrator. |
Brezenoff, Steven. Field trip mysteries.
Title: The disappearing fruit : an interactive mystery adventure / by
Steve Brezenoff ; illustrator Marcos Calo.
Other titles: You choose books.
Description: North Mankato, Minnesota : Stone Arch Books, a Capstone
imprint, [2017] | Series: You choose stories. Field trip mysteries
|Summary: While their sixth-grade class is on a trip to the River
City Conservatory the four young detectives, Sam, Egg, Gum, and Cat,
investigate the theft of a rare fruit from the botanical garden, and it
is up to the reader to determine the course of their adventure.
Identifiers: LCCN 2016038061| ISBN 9781496526434 (library binding) |
ISBN 9781496526472 (pbk.) | ISBN 9781496526519 (ebook (pdf))
Subjects: LCSH: School field trips—Juvenile fiction. | Botanical
gardens—Juvenile fiction. | Theft—Juvenile fiction. | School field trips—
stories.| CYAC: Mystery and detective stories. | Stealing—Fiction. | Plot-your-own
Fiction. | Botanical gardens—Fiction. | Plot-your-own
own stories. | GSAFD: Mystery fiction. | LCGFT: Detective and mystery
fiction.Classification: LCC PZ7.B7576 Dk 2017 | DDC 813.6 [Fic] —dc23

LC record available at https://lccn.loc.gov/2016038061

Graphic Designer: Kristi Carlson
Editor: Megan Atwood
Production Artist: Laura Manthe

Summary: After a rare fruit is stolen from the River City Botanical
Garden during a field trip, junior detectives Sam, Egg, Gum, and Cat
are on the case!

Printed in Canada.
010050S17

YOU CHOOSE STORIES

A FIELD TRIP MYSTERIES ADVENTURE

The DISAPPEARING Fruit

STONE ARCH BOOKS
a capstone imprint

Catalina Duran

A.K.A.: Cat

BIRTHDAY: February 15t'

LEVEL: 6th Grade

INTERESTS:

Animals, being "green

field trips

Edward G. Garrison

A.K.A.: Egg

BIRTHDAY: May 14th

LEVEL: 6th Grade

INTERESTS:

Photography, field trips

James Shoo

A.K.A.: Gum

BIRTHDAY: November 19th

LEVEL: 6th Grade

INTERESTS:
Gum-chewing, field trips, and showing everyone what a crook Anton Gutman is

Samantha Archer

A.K.A.: Sam

BIRTHDAY: August 20th

LEVEL: 6th Grade

INTERESTS:
Old movies, field trips

FIELD TRIP 🚌 MYSTERIES

Mr. Spade's sixth-grade class arrives at the River City Conservatory just after ten a.m. James Shoo — better known as Gum — is the first of his group of friends to reach the central lobby.

The circular atrium is well lit through its glass dome top. It's surrounded on all sides by glass-walled corridors. "They're like spider legs," Gum says about the outstretched greenhouses.

"I *love* this place," says Catalina Duran. "My dad used to bring me here during the long winters when I was little, so I'd have someplace warm to run around."

Samantha Archer steps between Cat and Gum and crosses her arms. She sighs, sounding something like a growling panther. "Sorry," she says, "but I'm *already* bored."

"Not me," says Edward Garrison, better known as Egg.

TURN THE PAGE.

He pats the camera dangling from the strap around his neck. "Some of the flowers in the tropics wing are very rare — and in bloom. I'll get lots of great photos."

While Mr. Spade talks to the conservatory guide, the four friends wander near the windows and look out over the snow-covered lawn and empty reflecting pool.

"In the summer, it's very lovely," Cat assures her friends.

"I'm sure," Sam says, turning around. "What's that?"

The others turn around too. Sam points at something on the floor. It looks like a purple rubber handball that's been cut in half.

Cat picks it up and sniffs it.

"Gross," Gum says.

"No, it smells good," Cat says. She holds it out to her friends. "See?"

"You mean smell," Gum says, sniffing it. "Fruit."

"So someone ate some fruit and left the rind on the floor," Sam says. "Ooh, crime of the century."

"It's very rude," Cat says as she walks toward the trash can near the door.

"Oh, my!" the conservatory guide says. Like a shot, he zips across the lobby, leaving Mr. Spade with his mouth hanging open.

The guide snatches the rind out of Cat's fingers. "Where," he says, his face wrinkled and red with rage, "did you get this, young lady?"

As her three best friends hurry to her side, Cat's face goes red and her eyes fill with tears. "I — "

"Whoa," says Chloe Marshfield, a girl from Mr. Spade's class, as she steps next to Cat and the guide. "Isn't that the rind of a mangosteen fruit? You can't even get those in the United States, can you?"

"*We* have a mangosteen tree in our tropics wing!" the guide says. "It's the only one in the northern United States. You'd have to fly to Hawaii for a mangosteen this fresh!"

TURN THE PAGE.

"I'd love one of those," Chloe says, practically salivating as she stares at the rind. She runs a hand through her short, dyed-blue hair. "Fruit is the *best*."

With that, Chloe walks off.

"I'll be telling your teacher about this," the guide says, looking squarely at Cat. "Children today have no respect for the rules."

The tears in Cat's eyes spill down her cheeks.

"She just picked it up off the floor," Gum says, stepping in front of Cat. "Someone else dropped it."

The guide squashes the rind in his fist so the dark juice runs between his fingers and stomps off.

"That was intense," Sam says after a beat. "Maybe this place isn't so boring after all."

Egg elbows her.

"Oh, sorry," Sam says, putting an arm around Cat. "It's all right. That guy's off his rocker."

"Guess we'd better find out who really dropped that fruit rind," Gum says, "if only to repair Cat's good name."

Just then, a short man in brown coveralls walks up to them. He is limping slightly. On his chest pocket in yellow thread it reads, *River City Conservatory* and under that, *DAN, VOLUNTEER.*

The man wipes his chin with a napkin, balls it up, and throws it in the trashcan. Then he pulls another napkin from his pocket and hands it to Cat. "Here you go," he says.

"Th-thanks," Cat says, dabbing at the tears on her cheeks.

The man nods, turns, and shuffles away.

"Did you notice how he wiped his chin?" Sam says.

Egg nods and snaps a photo of the man as he disappears into an adjacent greenhouse.

"All right, everyone," Mr. Spade says. "William's father, Mr. Hill, and I will be around if you need us, but feel free to wander off. Just stay on the paths and don't touch the plants!"

TO RUSH TO THE SCENE OF THE CRIME, TURN TO PAGE 12.
TO ASK CHLOE ABOUT THE STOLEN FRUIT, TURN TO PAGE 14.
TO HURRY AFTER THE VOLUNTEER, TURN TO PAGE 16.

Gum, Cat, Egg, and Sam rush to the tropics wing. "It looks okay to me," Gum says as they stand around the mangosteen tree.

The tree is small, but still one of the larger plants in the zone. Its leaves are deep green and shiny, and aside from a few purple spheres dangling, the tree seems unremarkable.

"That's because you don't know how to look," Sam says, dropping to one knee.

"Here," Sam says, pointing at a vague footprint in the dirt around the trunk. "And here."

Egg snaps some photos where Sam points. Just as he does, a group of Mr. Spade's students walk in with Mr. Hill.

At the back of the small pack are Anton Gutman and his two goons, Hans and Luca.

Anton, never able to resist trading insults with the junior detectives, strides right up to the four friends, Hans and Luca flanking him like burly bodyguards.

Anton grips a wrinkled paper bag in one hand.

"Well, well," he says. "A bunch of *nuts* and a bunch of fruit."

"I don't get it," Gum says.

"Nuts," Anton says as he reaches into the paper bag, "as in weirdos, like you and your nerd squad." He pulls out a mini candy bar, unwraps it, and pops it into his mouth. Then he drops the wrapper onto the path.

"Why are you always so *rude*?" Cat says as she picks up Anton's litter. "The garbage is like ten feet away!"

Anton and his goons laugh as they walk off.

Mr. Hill walks up to the mangosteen tree. "Did you hear about the stolen mangosteen fruit?"

The kids nod.

"Such a shame," Mr. Hill goes on. "Fine specimen. I hope the thief didn't damage it."

TO FOLLOW ANTON TO QUESTION HIM AND HIS GOONS, TURN TO PAGE 18.
TO FOLLOW MR. HILL AND ASK HIM ABOUT THE CRIME, TURN TO PAGE 25.

"I think she went in there," Cat says, pointing toward the door marked *Southwest United States and Mexico*.

"Let's go," Sam says, heading for the door. "She's up to something."

Chloe isn't hard to find. Among the muted colors of cactus and sand, her bright blue hair stands out like a tropical bird. She's sitting on a bench, hunched over the sketchbook in her lap.

Cat sits beside Chloe on the bench. "Shouldn't you be with a group?" Cat asks, her eyes wide and her eyebrows high.

Chloe doesn't even look up from her drawing. She replies, "Shouldn't *you*?"

"She is," Sam says, sitting on Chloe's other side. "Wise guy."

Chloe glances up at her and smirks.

"Wise gal?" Sam tries.

Chloe shrugs. "Look, I know why you're here," she says.

"Do you?" Gum says, crossing his arms and

blocking Chloe's view of the cactus she's sketching.

"Yup," Chloe says. "You think I stole the mangosteen fruit, and you're either going to question me or accuse me outright."

"Um," Cat says. "How — "

"You four are pretty clever," Chloe says, "but we artists are always watching, listening — a bit like you detectives, I bet."

Sam shifts on the bench. "You like fruit a lot."

"Everyone does," Chloe says.

"I don't," Gum says.

"You chew a lot of fruit-flavored gum," Chloe says.

"Ah, but that's fruit *flavor*," Gum says, proud.

"Look, it wasn't me," Chloe says. She closes her sketchbook and sticks her pencil behind her ear. "Ask Mr. Hill about it. That guy loves fruit as much as I do. He owns a fruit store."

With that, Chloe rises from the bench and hurries away.

To talk to Mr. Hill, turn to page 21.
To follow Chloe, turn to page 27.

The four friends hurry into the first greenhouse in the tropics wing. The short man in brown coveralls is not hard to catch up to.

"Shh," Sam hisses when she spots the volunteer walking along the path up ahead. She and her friends slow down and keep their distance.

"Look," Egg says. "He's holding something."

"It's a paper bag," Cat says.

"Kind of early for lunch," Gum says.

"Cat," Sam says quietly, "you only found the rind from *half* a mangosteen fruit, right?"

Cat nods.

"So the crook might still have the other half," Gum says. "Good thinking."

The volunteer continues to the next greenhouse.

"Hurry," Sam says when the door ahead closes.

The four sleuths move into the next greenhouse too. The volunteer is up ahead with his back to them, sitting on the edge of a little pond. The paper bag is in his lap.

"Take cover," Sam whispers. She and her friends hide behind thick ferns and bushes.

The man in brown unfolds the top of his paper bag and reaches in.

"What is it?" Cat whispers to Sam, beside her. "I can't see."

She doesn't have to wonder long. Whatever it is, the man brings it to his mouth and takes a big, juicy bite.

"It's a piece of fruit!" Cat declares.

Sam's mouth curves into a wicked smile. "He's busted," she says. "Easiest case ever."

Gum steps out from his cover. "Let's get him, then," he says.

"No!" Cat snaps, grabbing his wrist. "Let's go get Mr. Spade and the tour guide. This guy gives me the creeps. I don't want to confront him!"

"He might be dangerous," Sam says thoughtfully.

"Oh, come on," Gum says. "He's tiny — shorter than me and Sam. What could happen?"

TO CONFRONT THE VOLUNTEER, TURN TO PAGE 23.
TO GET MR. SPADE, TURN TO PAGE 29.

"It could be Anton, for sure. Which way did they go?" Sam asks as she leads her crew of junior detectives into the next greenhouse zone. It's a touch less humid and a bit cooler than the previous zone.

The sleuths move quietly down the central path until it forks. There, they decide to split up, Gum and Cat heading left, Egg and Sam heading right.

Both teams of two tiptoe among the greenery. Before long, both groups spot Anton and his goons sitting on a bench in the central patio between their two paths. The low bench circles a small pond's stone ledge.

Between the fat leaves of a coral tree, the three troublemakers open a paper bag and pull something out. Their sinister laughter echoes through the greenhouse.

Egg snaps a bunch of photos, but he can't make out what they have.

Sam signals to Gum across the patio, and the four sleuths meet up back at the exit.

"It might just have been more candy bars," Egg says.

"Or it might have been another banjo stein fruit," Gum says, nodding sagely.

"Mangosteen," Cat corrects him. "And I think we should go straight to Mr. Spade."

"You *always* think we should go straight to Mr. Spade," Sam says, crossing her arms and smirking.

"I do not." Cat's cheeks redden.

Gum shakes his head and glances back toward the little pond. "No way," he says. "They have the evidence we need in that bag. Let's bust 'em now."

To confront Anton and his goons and accuse them of the crime, turn to page 32.

To tell Mr. Spade Anton is the fruit-tree vandal, turn to page 48.

The four sleuths find Mr. Hill and his son — nicknamed Wild Bill — in the first greenhouse of the tropics zone.

"Come on," Sam says, striding right up to Mr. Hill.

The tree Mr. Hill is standing near and lecturing about is the mangosteen tree itself.

Gum opens his mouth to start firing questions at Mr. Hill. But before he can get out a word, Sam elbows him in the ribs.

"Ow!" Gum whispers, glaring at Sam and rubbing his side. "What'd you do that for?"

"Shh," she whispers back. "Just let him talk. If we give him enough rope, he might hang himself."

Cat shivers. "What a terrible expression."

"The mangosteen truly is a treasure," Mr. Hill says, as if lecturing in a university auditorium.

"While the off-putting durian is known as the king of fruits," Mr. Hill goes on, "its more palatable cousin the mangosteen is the undisputed queen."

Mr. Hill stares at the dangling fruits, smiling.

TURN THE PAGE.

Sam calls out, "What's it taste like?"

"Well," Mr. Hill says, "It's like a mix of vanilla ice cream, peaches, and strawberries."

"Ha!" says a voice from behind the four sleuths.

Slouching on the bench nearby is the volunteer.

"You don't know anything about mangosteen!" he says as his face reddens.

Sam and Egg exchange a glance.

"See here," Mr. Hill begins to reply, but the volunteer walks away in a huff. Mr. Hill keeps going anyway. "I own Hill's Grocery, a produce stand on Old Main Street. My father owned it before me, and his father before him. But," he goes on, "we don't sell the mangosteen. Someday, perhaps."

Mr. Hill walks off down the path. Wild Bill follows.

Egg snaps a photo of the tree. "We might need this later," he says.

Sam nods. "But it seems like we have two likely suspects."

TO ACCUSE THE VOLUNTEER, TURN TO PAGE 34.
TO ACCUSE MR. HILL, TURN TO PAGE 52.

"Okay," Sam says. "On 'three.' One, two, *three!*"

The four sleuths burst out from their hiding spot.

The volunteer's eyes go wide and he gasps.

Sam steps right up to him. "Hand it over!" she commands.

"Hand *what* over?" the volunteer says. He holds up a half-eaten, juicy pear. "This?"

"That's not the stolen fruit!" Cat whispers urgently.

The volunteer rises to his feet. "I'll teach you kids to frighten people like that!"

"Run!" Gum says.

The four friends don't stop running until they've crossed the next greenhouse and hidden behind some ferns.

"I think we lost him," Gum says, breathless.

But a moment later, the door to the greenhouse opens.

"Is it him?" Cat whispers.

TURN THE PAGE.

Sam takes a peek. "It's Mr. Hill," she says. "And some kids. Wild Bill, Anton Gutman . . . and his henchmen, of course."

"Stay hidden," Gum says. "If the volunteer isn't the crook, I bet Anton is."

Anton and his henchmen, Hans and Luca, step away from the group. Anton pulls out a paper bag and opens it.

"I knew it!" Gum says. "Let's bust 'em."

"You were wrong last time!" Cat points out.

Soon Anton and his goons walk away, cackling.

Sam leads her friends out of their hiding place.

Egg snaps a few photos while Sam checks out the soil for clues.

"What's up?" It's Wild Bill, Mr. Hill's son. "My dad knows everything about that tree," he says, not waiting for an answer. "He's been talking about it all month. That's why he's chaperoning this trip."

With that, he bounces off after his father.

TO TELL MR. SPADE THEY THINK ANTON AND HIS GOONS HAVE THE STOLEN FRUIT, TURN TO PAGE 36.

TO TELL MR. SPADE THAT THEY THINK MR. HILL IS THE VANDAL AND THIEF, TURN TO PAGE 55.

"Right this way, children," Mr. Hill says as he leads his son and the four junior detectives into the next greenhouse. "This zone mimics the climate of Hawaii."

Egg snaps a photo of the flowering little tree Mr. Hill stops next to. His son, Wild Bill Hill, stops beside him, a lollipop jutting from his lips.

"Here we have the strawberry guava," Mr. Hill says, stopping in front of a short, wild-looking tree with two trunks and small red fruit. "It's not actually native to Hawaii, but is highly invasive and grows all over the mountains of Kauai."

"Are we sure Wild Bill's dad doesn't actually work here?" Egg whispers to his friends.

Gum whispers back, "He sure knows a lot about this place."

Sam and Cat exchange a glance.

"As the name implies," Mr. Hill goes on, smiling, "this little fruit tastes like a mix between a guava and a strawberry."

"Whatever that means," Gum mutters.

TURN THE PAGE.

Mr. Hill closes his eyes and adds, "So delicious," as if savoring the memory. "Ah!" he goes on, striding deeper into the greenhouse. "The poha berry!"

When he and his son are out of earshot, the four sleuths huddle up.

Suddenly Gum elbows Sam.

"What?" Sam asks.

Gum nods toward a nearby bench. The volunteer in the brown jumpsuit sits there, a metal toothpick in his mouth, watching the four junior detectives.

Gum shakes his head. "Strange," he whispers. Then he changes topics. "Mr. Hill sure is good at describing what fruit tastes like," Gum says, eyeing the chaperone. "As if he just ate some."

"It didn't look like anything had been stolen from that little tree," Cat says.

"We might not be expert enough to spot any relevant clues," Sam says, shoving her hands into the pockets of her jeans. "And if Mr. Hill stole one of these, he's obviously capable of committing a crime."

TO ACCUSE MR. HILL OF HAVING TAKEN A FRUIT FROM THE SECOND TREE, TURN TO PAGE 68.

TO ASK MR. HILL WHY HE KNOWS SO MUCH ABOUT FRUIT, TURN TO PAGE 86.

The four sleuths watch Chloe walk into the first greenhouse of the tropics zone.

Cat wrinkles her face and twists her mouth.

"Cat," Sam says, crossing her arms. "We *know* that face. You have something to say and you think maybe you shouldn't say it."

Cat sighs. "Fine," she says. "I think Chloe Marshfield is a little bit . . . can sometimes be . . . kind of . . ."

Her face goes red.

"Annoying?" Gum says.

"Weird?" Egg says.

"Goofy?" Sam says.

Cat shakes her head. "Difficult."

"And suspicious," Sam says. "See the way she split? Hinky."

"Yep. Suspicious. So let's follow her," Gum says.

It doesn't take long to track her down. The four sleuths move into the first greenhouse and spot Chloe immediately.

TURN THE PAGE.

To their surprise, she steps over the little guard rope that runs along the paths to keep visitors off the soil and plants.

"What is she doing?" Gum whispers while Egg snaps a few photos.

"She may be difficult," Cat says, "but I really didn't think she'd be the crook. Isn't she a vegan?"

"So?" Gum says. "They eat fruit."

Cat shrugs. "But they should be so *ethical*."

Chloe leans closer to the nearest tree, peering at the gleaming purple fruit as if trying to see inside it.

"That's the mangosteen tree!" Cat says. "She's returning to the scene of the crime!"

After a moment — and without taking any fruit — Chloe hops the rope again and hurries along, toward the next greenhouse.

"Then we have proof," Gum says. "Let's take the photos to Mr. Spade."

"I want to take a closer look at the crime scene," Sam says.

TO GO TO MR. SPADE WITH THE PHOTO OF CHLOE, TURN TO PAGE 71.
TO CHECK OUT THE SCENE OF THE CRIME, TURN TO PAGE 89.

"Once Mr. Spade knows it wasn't you," Sam says as she and her friends hurry toward the lobby, "he'll tell the tour guide."

"I hope you're right, Sam," Cat says. "I hate knowing someone thinks I'm a bad kid."

On the way to the lobby, the four sleuths zip along the paths of the tropics wing. "There it is!" Cat says as they pass the mangosteen tree again.

"Egg," Sam says, skidding to a stop in front of it. "Might as well take some photos. We might need them later."

Egg flashes a thumbs-up and starts snapping photos. Behind them, someone clears her throat and says, "Excuse me?"

The four friends turn around and find Chloe Marshfield sitting on the bench behind them, farther along the path. She has a sketchpad on her lap and a pencil in her hand. She tosses her head to get her blue hair out of her face.

TURN THE PAGE.

"You're blocking my view," she says.

"Of what?" Gum says.

"The tree," Chloe says. She holds up her pad. "I'm drawing it."

"Hey, that's pretty good," Cat says, smiling.

"Thanks!" Chloe says as she sticks the pencil in her mouth. She picks at something between her front two teeth with it.

Sam grimaces. "Gross," she mutters. Then she asks, "Got something in your teeth?"

"Yeah," Chloe says. "Always happens when I eat *fruit*." She waggles her eyebrows at Sam. Then she goes back to her drawing.

Cat and Sam rejoin Gum and Egg at the mangosteen tree.

"OK," Egg says, "I think I got enough photos."

"Let's go talk to Mr. Spade," Cat says.

"Chloe is acting suspicious," Sam says. "Maybe we should question her."

To question Chloe, turn to page 73.
To hurry on to Mr. Spade, turn to page 92.

The four sleuths crouch at the north end of the greenhouse.

"They're still there," Gum says. "Let's charge them!"

"And give them a chance to hide the evidence?" Sam says. "No way. We'll split up again and block their exits."

"You're the boss," Cat says.

"She is?" Gum says, standing up. "Since when?"

"Shh," Egg hisses, pulling Gum by the wrist down to a crouch again. "Gum and I will block the left. Girls, you take the right."

Sam and Cat nod.

"If we're quiet, they won't have a chance to dump the bag," Sam says. "If they hear us, we'll never get the proof we need to bring to Mr. Spade and the tour guide who spooked Cat earlier."

"All right," Gum says, narrowing his eyes and setting his jaw. "Let's do this."

The detectives creep along the outside paths. The only sound in the greenhouse is the hum of the filtration system, the crinkle of the troublemakers' paper bag, and Anton's occasional laughter.

Just outside the patio, the four sleuths hide out of sight of the troublemakers but still in sight of each other.

Sam raises three fingers and mouths a countdown: *Three, two, one . . . Now!*

The four friends pounce onto the patio, blocking the exits and stunning Anton and his goons, freezing them in place for an instant.

It's long enough for Gum to snatch away the paper bag and hold it up. "Aha!" he gloats. "We caught you red-handed!"

"What?" Anton says, rising from the bench. His goons rise, too, and stand beside him. "With a bag of old Halloween candy bars?"

"You stole the mangosteen fruit," Gum says. "And we saw you three laughing about it just a couple of minutes ago."

TURN TO PAGE 38.

"It has to be that volunteer," Egg says. "Did you hear how sure he was about what mangosteen fruit tastes like?"

"He's our man," Sam says. "He sure sounded like someone who had just eaten a mangosteen."

"I'm convinced," Gum says, popping a piece of blueberry gum into his mouth. "So where'd he go?"

"In there, I think," Egg says, pointing to the next greenhouse.

The four friends walk to the next house and find the volunteer sweeping the brick path. No one else is around, and the volunteer is very absorbed in his work.

When the four sleuths walk up to him, he doesn't even notice.

Gum coughs. Nothing.

"Excuse us," Cat says.

The volunteer looks up from his broom. "Oh," he says. "I didn't see you. Am I blocking the path?"

"Oh, no," Cat says, smiling. "We wanted to talk to you."

The man smiles as he sits on the nearby bench. "Any excuse for a break," he says, grinning. "What can I do for you?"

"Look, Mac," Sam says. "You're made. Nailed. Set up and knocked down. We've got you dead to rights."

The volunteer looks at Cat.

"Um," she says, giving Sam a little shove, "we were just wondering, how do you know mangosteen fruit so well?"

"What do you mean?" the man asks, leaning forward on the bench.

Gum explains, "You said Mr. Hill didn't know what he was talking about. But you do?"

"Ah," the volunteer says. "It was long ago now, but for twenty years of my life, I lived in Thailand, teaching. That's where the mangosteen is from. I ate them all the time back then!"

He smiles a sad sort of smile.

"I haven't had a mangosteen in many years," he goes on, his voice gentle and faraway.

TURN TO PAGE 42.

"Mr. Spade!" Gum says as he leads the group of junior detectives into the first greenhouse of the boreal forest wing.

The teacher is clear across the quiet greenhouse with a group of their classmates. Gum's shouting shatters the silence.

Mr. Spade looks up and pulls off his glasses.

"What are you shouting about?" he asks. "And why are you four running in the conservatory?"

The four sleuths slow to a jog as they cross a little bridge over a small brook.

"Is someone hurt?" asks Chloe Marshfield, who sits on a bench nearby. Her sketchpad is in her lap, and she holds a pencil just above the paper. They obviously interrupted her drawing.

"What?" Gum says. "No. Mr. Spade, we know who the crook is!"

Mr. Spade sighs. "James Shoo," he says, and then looks at the other detectives. "And you three, too. Can't we just enjoy a nice day at the conservatory without the police showing up?"

Chloe rises from the bench, sticks her sketchbook under one arm, and strolls over. "They're talking about the stolen fruit," she says. "I hope they don't think I did it!"

"You?" Cat says. "Why would we think that?"

Chloe shrugs. "I think *you* did it," she says, looking right at Cat.

"Okay, okay," Mr. Spade says, putting up both hands to quiet the students. "What is this all about?"

"Easy," Chloe says. "Catalina stole that mangosteen fruit, and now she's trying to blame someone else."

"Why I oughta . . . ," Sam says, snarling at Chloe. Gum and Egg hold her back while Chloe strolls away, chuckling.

"It's not like that, Mr. Spade," Cat says. "Honest!"

"Cat," Mr. Spade says, "you're the last person I'd suspect of stealing or lying."

Turn to page 45.

"And I got yelled at for it," Cat adds.

Anton opens his mouth to answer, but instead of speaking he just doubles over laughing.

"What's so funny?" Gum says, his face going hot.

"Someone stole some weird hippie fruit," Anton says, "and you think it was *us*?"

Gum peers into the bag. He sticks his hand in and fishes around, but only finds mini candy bars and some empty wrappers.

"Um," he says, forcing a smile as he looks up at Anton, Luca, and Hans. "No hard feelings, right?"

He backs up a bit.

"Hard feelings?" Anton says. "I don't *do* hard feelings."

"Oh, good," Gum says, relaxing a little and handing over the bag.

Anton grabs it and sits down again. He pulls out a little Choco-mellow bar and unwraps it slowly. "Hans and Luca," he says calmly, "they do my hard feelings for me. Boys."

"Whoa, whoa," Gum says, backing away as the two goons approach him. "Whatever he's paying you, I'll double it."

Sam steps in front of him. "Stop right there," she says. "No need for a scene."

Luca and Hans exchange a glance. Then they each take Sam by an arm, lift her up off the patio, and carry her to the pond's edge.

"Put her down!" Cat shrieks.

"Are you nuts?" Gum says, grabbing Luca's wrist.

Luca stops and turns, still dangling Sam inches from the water.

"Today," Luca says, "your friend sleeps with the fishes."

Sam's eyes go wide. "Please tell me you don't know what that *really* means," she says.

The goons let go, and she lands on her feet in 18 inches of cold water. Koi swim between her ankles and nibble on her jeans.

TURN THE PAGE.

Anton rolls off the bench, laughing.

At the same moment, Mr. Spade and a group of their classmates step onto the patio. "What's going . . . " Mr. Spade says, and then he spots Sam in the pond. "Samantha Archer, what in the name of all that is holy do you think you're doing?"

Five minutes later, the four sleuths are sitting together in the little office just off the conservatory's main lobby, the director watching them from his desk, a stern look on his face.

Sam's jeans drip on the carpet.

"That didn't go so well," Egg says. He's already taken ten photos of Sam — in the pond, climbing out of the pond, dripping on the carpet — but he takes one more as she glowers at him.

"And we didn't solve the case," Cat points out. "Now we're stuck here till the field trip is over."

THE END

TO FOLLOW ANOTHER PATH, TURN TO PAGE 11.

Egg sits beside the volunteer on the bench. "Maybe this morning you were feeling," Egg says, "a little nostalgic?"

The volunteer gives Egg a funny look, and then looks at Sam again. "You kids think I stole the mangosteen earlier!" he says, standing suddenly.

"Admit it!" Sam says, putting her fists on her hips. "You couldn't handle the temptation anymore!"

"I didn't do it!" the volunteer insists, leaning away from his accuser.

"'Fess up, meat!" Sam snarls.

"But I'm telling you!" the volunteer says. "I've done nothing wrong!"

"Where were you this morning at 8:45?" Sam snaps.

The volunteer flinches. "I-I don't know!"

"Wait a second!" Egg says, rising from the bench and pulling off his camera. "Look at this."

He clicks on the display and holds it out to Sam. "Right there," Egg says.

"It's the mangosteen tree," Sam says. "So?"

Egg taps the zoom button a few times. "Right there," Egg says again.

Sam squints at the display. Her mouth bends into a grin. "Footprints."

She whispers to Egg, "Now I'll intimidate him into confessing. The police do this all the time."

Sam, grinning, turns the display so he can see it. "Right there. I bet that's your footprint!"

"But . . . but," the volunteer says, "Those are *not* my footprints."

"How can you be so sure?" Sam asks.

The volunteer closes his eyes and smiles. "Those are work boot prints. I wear gardening clogs, all day, every day," he says.

Everyone looks at his feet. Sure enough, he's wearing rubber shoes. Definitely *not* work boots.

TURN THE PAGE.

"You probably changed your shoes!" Sam says. But under her breath she mutters, "Darn, I was sure that would work."

The volunteer grabs his broom and starts sweeping again, smiling as he works. "Looks like you four are barking up the wrong tree!"

Gum laughs. "He used Sam's funny words on Sam!" he says.

"All right, all right," Sam says. "That'll teach me to accuse someone before reviewing the evidence. Back to the drawing board."

THE END

TO FOLLOW ANOTHER PATH, TURN TO PAGE 11.

Mr. Spade continues, "So, why don't you four tell me what you know?"

"We saw Anton Gutman," Gum says, "and his two meathead friends with the stolen fruit."

Mr. Spade's eyes go wide. "You actually saw it?"

Gum shrugs. "We saw them with a paper bag."

Mr. Spade raises his eyebrows and looks at Egg.

"They were laughing," Egg says.

Mr. Spade turns to Sam.

"More like cackling," Sam adds.

Mr. Spade turns to Cat.

Cat's face turns red. "Um," she says, "they seemed pretty suspicious to me."

Just then, Mr. Hill comes into the Northern Forest greenhouse. At his heels are his son, Wild Bill, and Anton and his two goons, Luca and Hans.

Everyone turns to look at them.

"What?" Anton says, stopping. His two goons bump right into him. "Watch it, you gorillas."

TURN THE PAGE.

"Anton Gutman," Mr. Spade says, striding right up to him, "did you have a paper bag you were holding just recently?"

"What paper bag?" Anton asks, grinning. He is obviously enjoying himself.

"These four say you had a paper bag," Mr. Spade says, "with a stolen mangosteen fruit in it."

Anton shrugs. "I don't see a bag, do you?"

Mr. Spade says, "Mr. Hill, was Anton carrying anything?"

Mr. Hill says, "To be honest, I wasn't paying attention. Bill?" Wild Bill shrugs and continues walking in circles around some greenery.

Anton puts on an innocent look. "Mr. Spade, those four have it out for me. I think they should be in trouble for falsely accusing me! Cat just wants to blame someone else for what she did." He grins an evil grin at Cat when Mr. Spade and Mr. Hill aren't looking.

Mr. Spade furrows his brow. "What do you have to say about that, Catalina?"

"That's not true!" Cat says.

"Think about it, Mr. Spade. Like I'd steal fruit," Anton says. "I don't even eat fruit when I'm supposed to. You think I'm going to *steal* some?"

Mr. Spade looks at Cat. "It's hard to argue with that, Cat."

"Can I go now?" Anton asks, keeping his eyes wide and innocent. Mr. Spade sighs and nods. Anton and his goons walk away, snickering.

Cat blows out air. "That was humiliating. It wasn't me, Mr. Spade. I swear." Sam puts her arm around Cat's shoulders.

"I don't doubt that, Cat. But next time you'd better have some proof before you accuse anyone else."

THE END

TO FOLLOW ANOTHER PATH, TURN TO PAGE 11.

"I think Cat's right," Egg says. "I got a few photos of those three and their bag. We can show Mr. Spade. It might be enough."

Sam and Gum exchange a glance. "All right," Sam says. "Let's go find Mr. Spade."

Cat smiles. "I saw him head into the cooler climate wing, back through the lobby."

The four friends head for the exit, toward the center of the conservatory. As they do, a low-hanging branch full of bright red flowers brushes Sam's nose.

And she sneezes.

Loudly.

Three times.

The three goons at the koi pond look up from their bag and spot Sam, Cat, Gum, and Egg trying to sneak away. The four sleuths freeze — getting Anton's attention is always a bad idea.

"What are you nerds doing?" Anton shouts, rising from the bench. His goons rise beside him.

"Uh-oh," Gum says. "Let's move."

Sam nods, grabs Cat's hand, and takes off for the exit. Egg and Gum run close behind.

"They're up to something!" Anton shouts. "After them!"

The four friends dart across the tropics wing, zigzagging along the winding paths between exotic trees and flowers, across little wooden bridges over bubbling artificial brooks.

The pounding footsteps of Luca and Hans echo through the greenhouse as they and Anton charge after them.

"They must know we saw them with the mangosteen!" Cat says as she and her friends run past the short man in the brown jumpsuit.

He sits on a wooden bench at the side of the path and watches the kids run by, shaking his head.

The sleuths shove through the glass doors and into the central atrium of the conservatory. It's empty now.

"This way!" Cat says, leading her friends through the door marked *Northern Climes*.

TURN THE PAGE.

The temperature drops at once. The air is full of the smell of pine needles and frost.

"Are — you — shh-sure — Mr. — Spade — came — this — w-w-way?" Sam asks, shivering in her T-shirt.

Egg grabs Sam's arm to pull her along. He's wearing long sleeves, and the chill doesn't bother him as much.

"I saw him pull on his parka," Cat says. "He must have come this way."

The four friends hurry along the path, ducking under jutting conifer limbs. The brook here is frozen, but just under the ice, fish are swimming.

There's no sign of Mr. Spade.

"Next zone!" Cat says, pulling open the door for her friends.

Gum, Egg, and Sam hurry into the Temperate Zone. Cat follows, letting the door close behind her.

As it closes, she spots Anton and his goons not far behind.

"Hurry!" Cat shouts. "They're right behind us!"

TURN TO PAGE 58.

"I'm telling you guys," Sam says as she leads her crew of sleuths through the central lobby. "I make the volunteer for our crook."

"Sam," Egg says, "look at the facts. Mr. Hill knows and loves fruit."

"More importantly," Cat says, "he *sells* fruit. And it's like you always say about cracking a case, Sam."

Sam nods and smirks. "I know, I know," she says. "'Follow the money.'"

"Exactly," Cat says. She pulls open the door for her friends, and they all enter the Northern Forest greenhouse.

"Even so," Egg says, "we'll need some proof. A hunch about Mr. Hill's business doesn't get us very far."

"Right," Cat says. "Mr. Spade gets so irritable when we go around blaming parents for crimes."

"And I don't want to spend the rest of the day on the bus with Smelly Mel," Gum says, shivering, "while he chomps on an egg salad sandwich with extra pickles. Blech."

Sam hugs herself to fight the chill in the greenhouse. "Then let's find some proof," she says.

The four friends huddle together on a bench and look through all of Egg's photos. Sam pulls out her notebook to check her notes. Then she looks back at Egg's photos.

"I have to check something out in the tropics," Sam says, getting up.

"Want us to come?" Cat says.

"No, I'll be fine," Sam says. "Wait here. Won't be long."

With that, she sprints from the chilly greenhouse and into the lobby.

Sam hurries across the lobby. The volunteer pushes a cart loaded with plastic sacks of soil.

Sam glances at his feet: *gardening clogs*. She smiles and hurries on.

She hurries into the tropics wing. The heat wraps itself around her like a wet blanket.

Sam's whole body relaxes as the chill of the northern wing fades.

TURN THE PAGE.

In the first greenhouse, Sam dashes past Anton and his two giant henchmen. She glances at them, watching them suspiciously as they root through a paper bag.

"What are you looking at, nerd?" Anton says.

Sneakers, Sam thinks as she checks their feet, and then runs on.

Around the bend, she finds Mr. Hill crouched next to a plant with bright orange and yellow flowers.

She takes a good look at Mr. Hill's shoes, *brown boots with a heavy tread*, and runs back to the chilly northern greenhouse.

"You guys," she says when she reaches her friends, "I think we've got him. Let me see those photos one more time."

Sam puts her fists on her hips as she catches her breath.

Egg turns on his camera's display. He clicks through the photos until he finds the images of the crime scene.

"Zoom in right there," Sam says.

TURN TO PAGE 62.

"Mr. Spade," Sam says as she crosses the little wooden bridge in the Northern Forest Zone. "I've cracked the case!"

Mr. Spade looks up from a juniper shrub. When he spots Sam coming off the bridge — with her crew of crime-crackers behind her — he pulls off his glasses and rubs his eyes.

"Hey," Gum says. "My dad does that when I'm really annoying and he's trying to read."

"Samantha Archer," Mr. Spade says when the four friends stop in front of him, "there is no case to crack. It's just a bunch of greenhouses. You should be choosing a favorite plant to present to the class on Monday."

"How can you think about a presentation at a time like this?" Sam says.

Mr. Spade sighs. "Fine," he says. "Fine. Tell me what crime you've solved."

"Cat didn't steal the mangosteen fruit," Gum says.

Mr. Spade says, "Are you referring to the rind of fruit Cat was holding this morning?"

TURN THE PAGE.

Gum grins. "It was Anton," he says.

"No, it wasn't," Sam says. "It was Wild Bill's dad, Mr. Hill."

"What?" Gum and Mr. Spade say at the same time.

"You heard me," Sam says. "And I can prove it."

"This I have to hear," Mr. Spade says.

Sam shakes her head. "This you have to *see*," she says.

At the same moment, Mr. Hill walks in, leading Wild Bill and Anton and his two goons.

"Ah, Mr. Hill," Mr. Spade says, calling over the group. "We were just talking about you."

"Is that right?" Mr. Hill says, glaring at the four sleuths.

"It sure is!" Sam says, putting on her best face to impress adults. It doesn't work. "Um, would you mind coming over to the first tropics greenhouse with us?" Sam asks.

"We just came from there," Mr. Hill says. "No, I think I'd rather stay here."

"Hmm," Sam says, rubbing her chin.

Suddenly her face brightens. "Oh!" she says. "I have an idea. You stay here and let me borrow your boots for a second."

She crouches as if to pull them right off his feet.

"What?" Mr. Hill says, stepping back. "I should say not! What is this all about?"

Mr. Spade rubs his eyes again. "It seems," he says to Mr. Hill, "that Samantha here believes you are guilty of a minor crime."

Mr. Hill narrows his eyes at Sam. "What crime am I supposed to have committed?"

"Stealing a fruit," Gum says. "No biggie, right?"

"Ridiculous," Mr. Hill says. "Besides, what does this have to do with my boots?"

"There are footprints at the scene of the crime," Sam says.

"There are?" Gum asks quietly.

"I spotted them just before Wild Bill came along," Sam explains.

Turn to page 65.

Now the air is like a crisp fall day. A sparrow — sometimes birds find their way into the conservatory — takes flight from an apple tree.

Sam, warmed up a bit, runs along the path. "There he is!" she calls to her friends as she crosses a little stone bridge. "Mr. Spade!"

Their teacher looks up. His parka is open. He pulls off his glasses and squints at Sam, Gum, Egg, and Cat as they hurry toward him.

"No running, please!" Mr. Spade says.

The four sleuths bump to a stop at his side. "Anton is chasing us," Cat explains.

"He stole the mangosteen fruit," Gum says. "Him and Luca and Hans."

"All of them?" Mr. Spade says.

Just then, the three troublemakers cross the stone bridge and slow down. They stroll up to Mr. Spade and the junior detectives.

Anton smirks, still gripping the paper bag in one hand. "I tried to tell them not to run, Mr. Spade," Anton says. "They wouldn't listen."

"Mm-hm," Mr. Spade says. "Is that right?"

"Actually," Cat says, "Anton was chasing us because of that bag."

Mr. Spade's eyebrows go up and he puts his glasses back on.

"Hand it over, Mr. Gutman," he says, putting out his hand.

Anton knots his brow, sighs, and rolls his eyes, but he hands over the bag.

Mr. Spade unrolls the top and peers in. "Candy bars?" he says. "You know you're not supposed to bring food into the conservatory greenhouses, Anton."

Anton shrugs. "I guess I forgot."

"I'll hold on to this," Mr. Spade says, rolling up the top. "And if the conservatory director tells me later that he found even one candy wrapper on the path, I'll know who to talk to."

Anton grumbles and glares at Cat and her friends. Hans and Luca growl like guard dogs.

TURN THE PAGE.

"You kids, try to get along, all right?" Mr. Spade says. "Now I'm going to enjoy the rest of the day."

With that, he moves on to the next zone.

"Snitches," Anton says, narrowing his eyes at Sam, Cat, Gum, and Egg.

Hans and Luca growl some more. "Our candy," Hans says.

"He took it," Luca grunts. He makes a fist.

"They're not worth it," Anton says. "Let's go. I think there's a vending machine in the lobby." With that, the three walk off.

"Better watch your step from now on!" Anton says over his shoulder.

Cat takes a deep breath. "That did not go well."

"We'd better try something else," Sam says, and she sits on the edge of the path and puts her chin on her knees.

THE END

To follow another path, turn to page 11.

Egg double-taps the display until it shows a section of the soil around the mangosteen tree.

Sam grins. "That's the rope that'll hang him."

At the far end of the greenhouse, a door flies open and Mr. Spade comes in with Chloe and a couple of other students from class. "And that's why it's called a boreal forest," he's saying.

Mr. Spade spots the four sleuths. "And what are you four up to?" he asks.

"Mr. Spade," Sam says. "We've cracked the case."

"Case?" Mr. Spade says. "And here I thought we'd managed to have a field trip without anyone committing a crime!"

Cat pipes up, "The stolen mangosteen fruit, remember?"

"Oh," Mr. Spade says, looking down his nose at her. "I thought *you'd* done that, Catalina."

Egg says. "Cat would never do that."

"Especially throwing the rind on the floor after," Gum says, shaking his head.

"I suppose you're right," Mr. Spade says. "I'm sorry, Cat. Who do you think did it?"

"Mr. Hill," Sam says.

Mr. Spade's eyes go wide as he says, "I hope you have some evidence to back up that claim."

"Or we'll spend the rest of the field trip on the bus with Smelly Mel," Gum adds in his silliest grownup voice.

Mr. Spade shoots him a disapproving look.

"Show him the photo, Egg," Sam says.

Egg pulls up the photo on his camera's display.

The teacher squints at the screen. "A footprint," he says. "From a boot."

The volunteer and his cart of soil arrive.

"Nice clogs," Sam says.

The volunteer glances at Mr. Spade as if to say, *What's up with her?*

"Can you tell me," Mr. Spade asks, "how often do you rake the soil?"

The man says, "Frequently."

TURN THE PAGE.

"I see," Mr. Spade says. "So if the soil is disturbed this morning, it's from my students or a chaperone?"

The volunteer nods. "That's right."

Just then, Mr. Hill and his son walk in from the lobby.

Mr. Spade sees Mr. Hill's boots and says, "Looks like you junior detectives are on to something."

"Thanks, Mr. Spade," Egg says. "And maybe speak to the tour guide too?"

Mr. Spade says, smiling,. "Consider it done."

"Thank you, Mr. Spade," Cat says. She turns to her friends and adds, "And especially thanks to you guys."

"Don't mention it," Sam says. "If a detective can't get her friend off the hook, what good is she? Now," she says, grinning determinedly at Mr. Hill, "let's serve some justice."

Mr. Hill takes a step back.

THE END

TO FOLLOW ANOTHER PATH, TURN TO PAGE 11.

"Mr. Hill," Mr. Spade says, "why don't we go over to the mangosteen tree and put this nonsense to rest."

"What?" Mr. Hill says. "Are you saying I must *prove* my innocence? I've never been so insulted."

"Well, it's early," Sam says.

The greenhouse door swings open again and the volunteer in the brown coveralls walks in. Over his shoulder he carries a bow rake.

Mr. Hill suddenly smiles. "Actually," he says, "why not? No harm in walking over there. It will clear this up once and for all."

Sam and Egg exchange a glance and a shrug. "All right," Sam says. "Follow me!"

A minute later, Sam, Egg, Cat, Gum, Mr. Spade, Mr. Hill, and Wild Bill stand in a half circle around the mangosteen tree.

The volunteer follows them, looking at the crowd of people curiously. "What's going on?" he asks. No one answers.

Sam frowns. "I don't understand this," she says. "Where'd the footprints go?"

TURN THE PAGE.

The soil around the mangosteen trunk is raked into a hundred perfect lines. Any sign of footprints has been erased.

"I raked 'em," the volunteer says. "Part of my job."

"Well, then," Mr. Hill says, his smile as wide as the whole outdoors. "I guess that's that. If there are no footprints to match, the whole point is moot."

"Just a second," Egg says, pulling off the camera from his neck. He clicks on the display and scrolls through the last few photos. "Here it is."

He holds out the display to Mr. Spade.

"I took this just before we went looking for you," he says.

"Is that . . . dirt?" Mr. Spade says.

Egg taps the zoom button.

"Oh, I see," Mr. Spade says.

Sam looks over his shoulder. "The footprint!" she exclaims. "Egg, you saved the day!"

Mr. Hill's face goes red and he backs away from the group. "I just remembered," he says. "I, um, have to make an urgent phone call, so I'd better . . ."

He turns to run — and trips right over the edge of the path, falling face-first into a shrub.

"Uh-oh," the volunteer says, leaning on the handle of his rake. "That's fever nettle."

Mr. Hill pushes himself up and immediately starts scratching. "It burns!" he shouts as the skin on his hands and face turns red. "And itches!"

"Probably don't touch your eyes," the volunteer says as Mr. Hill runs toward the bathroom.

"Cat," Mr. Spade says, "I'll let the conservatory guide know that you are not the crook he thought you were."

"Thanks, Mr. Spade," she says. She turns to Sam and Egg. "And thanks to you two, too. You sure caught him *red-handed*."

THE END

TO FOLLOW ANOTHER PATH, TURN TO PAGE 11.

"How should we accuse him?" Gum asks.

He and his friends stand back from Mr. Hill. Wild Bill paces behind his father, chomping on his bare lollipop stick.

"We have to get Wild Bill out of the way," Sam says. "Can't have any loose cannons who might throw a monkey wrench and gum up the works."

"I understood just one word of that," Gum says, "and that's only because it's my nickname."

"Just follow my lead," Sam says, and she strolls a little closer to Wild Bill.

Her three friends follow.

"So," Sam says to Cat, "did you hear about the ten-story climbing tree they have in the Northern Forest Zone, all the way on the other side of the conservatory?"

"Yeah," Cat says, glancing briefly at Wild Bill. "You can actually climb it."

"A kid from Obama Middle School got all the way to the top and they had to call the fire department to get her down," Gum says.

"Are you saying you're allowed to climb a giant tree," Wild Bill asks, looking from Cat to Gum to Sam, "and that a girl from our rival school got all the way to the top?"

Sam nods. "That's what we're saying."

Wild Bill glances at his distracted dad and then takes off in the direction of the Northern Forest Zone.

"That got rid of him," Egg says. "Nice going."

Sam grins. "He's an easy make," she says. "Now the big fish."

She steps up to Mr. Hill. Gum moves up beside her.

"So, Mr. Hill," Sam says. "You sure know a lot about the fruit here at the conservatory."

Mr. Hill stops his lecture and looks at Sam, his eyebrows high.

"You did a great job describing the strawberry guava plant," Gum says, "which I've never even heard of."

TURN TO PAGE 75.

Sam shakes her head as she, Egg, Cat, and Gum walk quickly through the central lobby.

"I don't know about this, guys," Sam says. "The photo is pretty convincing, but . . ."

"But what?" Egg says, flicking on his camera.

Sam smirks, and Gum explains, "It's not enough to really prove anything — it just makes it seem like Chloe is probably guilty."

"It's not enough," Sam says.

"It will be for Mr. Spade," Egg says.

"Besides, Chloe broke a rule, right?" Cat says.

"Cat," Sam says, "we're detectives, not tattletales."

Cat sulks and crosses her arms.

The four friends go into the Northern Forest Zone. The chill here is nothing compared with the chill among the four friends.

"There's Mr. Spade," Egg says.

He and Cat hurry ahead while Gum and Sam hang back.

TURN THE PAGE.

"Mr. Spade," Egg says. "We have some evidence you should see."

"What's the crime?" Mr. Spade asks.

"The stolen fruit!" Cat says.

Mr. Spade looks down his nose at Cat and lifts his eyebrows.

Egg shows him the photo. Mr. Spade squints at the camera's little display.

"Is that Chloe Marshfield?" he asks.

Cat and Egg nod.

"What is she doing?" Mr. Spade says. "She's not supposed to be doing that."

The teacher looks around and spots Chloe's bright blue hair clear across the greenhouse..

"Chloe Marshfield!" Mr. Spade calls.

The girl flinches, looking up from the sketchbook on her lap.

At the same moment, the tour guide arrives with a small group of students.

"Come here, please!" Mr. Spade calls to Chloe.

TURN TO PAGE 79.

"Let's start here," Sam says, crossing her arms and lowering her chin. "I'm not ready to move on quite yet."

She narrows her eyes, and her glare is like a laser beam across the greenhouse, right to Chloe Marshfield on the bench, sketching away in her pad.

"Why do you think Chloe did it?" Egg says.

"Point one," Sam says, "she's not just sitting there. She's just sitting *there* — only a few steps from the mangosteen tree, the scene of the crime. And what's the first rule of crime-solving?"

"Follow the money?" Gum tries.

Sam shakes her head.

"The postman always rings twice?" Egg says.

Sam shakes her head.

Cat suddenly snaps her fingers and says, "The crook always returns to the scene of the crime!"

Turn the page.

"You got it, Cat," Sam says. "Point two, she's got food in her teeth, as if she just ate a piece of fruit. She even *admitted* she just ate a piece of fruit."

"So we question her," Gum says. "Right?"

Sam nods, and the four friends walk up to Chloe's bench. Sam sits on one side of her and Gum sits on her other side. Egg and Cat stand a couple of paces back.

"So you just ate some fruit," Gum says.

"Yeah?" Chloe says.

"I hear you *love* fruit," Sam says.

Chloe shrugs.

"Love it enough," Sam adds, leaning closer to Chloe, "to *steal* it?"

"What are you saying?" Chloe asks, shrinking from Sam on the bench.

"You know what she's saying!" Gum says.

TURN TO PAGE 82.

"And you know a lot about these funny little poha berries too," Sam says.

"Which look like they're from another planet," Egg says.

Gum chuckles. "You know, they really ought to put up a sign so people know not to taste the fruit right off the trees here at the conservatory," he says.

Sam nods. "Yeah, you probably won't get in much trouble, though," she says, "if you say it was just an honest mistake."

"You think I tasted fruit from the trees?" Mr. Hill says. "That's ridiculous."

Cat moves quietly around Mr. Hill. The top zipper of his backpack is half open. Sticking out is the distinctive green stripe of a zip-top plastic bag.

"Aha!" Cat says, snatching the bag from the backpack.

Mr. Hill spins to stop her, but Cat is small and quick. She dodges and tosses the bag to Sam.

"What do we have here?" Sam says.

TURN THE PAGE.

"You give that back to me," Mr. Hill says. "Right now."

Sam tosses the bag to Egg.

"I don't know as much about these fruits as Mr. Hill does," Egg says, examining the plastic bag, "but this bag contains gauze and some seeds. Looks like someone wants to grow their own tree."

"And if we brought those to the conservatory staff," Cat says, "I bet they'd tell us those are mangosteen seeds."

Mr. Hill's eyes go wide. Suddenly, he drops onto a bench and puts his head in his hands.

"It's true, it's true!" he groans.

Egg immediately starts shooting video with his digital camera to catch the confession.

"After tasting the fruit, I had to have some of the seeds," Mr. Hill goes on. "I have my own greenhouse on the family farm."

"Family farm?" Egg says, surprised. "In River City?"

"The farm is upstate," Mr. Hill says, calming down. "We raise some of the produce for the store there. I'm a greengrocer. Didn't you know?"

The kids shake their heads.

"If I could raise a healthy mangosteen tree," Mr. Hill goes on, "in around ten years I'd have the only viable crop of mangosteen within a thousand miles. My store would be famous!"

"He's not raising fruits," Sam says. "He's raising *lettuce*." Sam looks around proudly.

Mr. Hill glances at Sam, confusion on his face.

Egg says to him, "Lettuce is old-fashioned slang for money," he says. "Sam's . . . eccentric."

"Well, I would have gotten away with it," Mr. Hill says, "if it weren't for you kids."

Cat takes the baggy from Egg. "I'll take these to the office," she says, "and explain the whole scheme. Someone owes me an apology."

THE END

TO FOLLOW ANOTHER PATH, TURN TO PAGE 11.

"What's the matter?" the tour guide asks, hurrying toward the teacher.

Chloe stands before them, her face eager and open, not an ounce of guilt on her face.

"Chloe," Mr. Spade, "do you know what the paths here at the conservatory are for?"

"Um," Chloe says, "walking on?"

"Then maybe you can explain why you thought *you* were allowed to walk on the soil," Mr. Spade says, "instead of the path?"

"Did I?" Chloe says.

"At the mangosteen tree," Mr. Spade says.

"Oh," Chloe says, her cheeks going red. "Right."

Cat and Egg exchange a glance as Sam and Gum move up beside them.

"I see what's going on here," the tour guide says. "You stole that fruit — the one your classmate found in the lobby earlier."

Chloe's eyes go wide. "No!" she says, her voice high and thin. "I didn't! I just wanted to get a closer look at the fruit for my sketch."

TURN THE PAGE.

Chloe pulls the sketchbook from her shoulder bag and flips through the pages. "Here," she says, holding up a recent sketch. "See?"

"Hey, that's pretty good," Egg says.

"Pretty good?" the tour guide says.

Chloe looks up at the tour guide as he stares at the drawing intently.

"In my opinion," the tour guide says, "this drawing is nothing short of . . . fantastic!"

"Say what now?" Chloe says.

"It's a beautiful work of art!" the tour guide says, snatching away the sketchbook and flipping through the other pictures. "And you have other drawings of the conservatory's collection!"

Chloe's mouth spreads into a huge grin. "Well, yeah," she says. "I've been drawing all morning."

"I must have these drawings," the guide says. "We'll frame them and hang them in the lobby, an installation for — what's your name?"

"Chloe Marshfield," Chloe says.

"The Chloe Marshfield art installation," the guide says. "It'll be marvelous."

He puts an arm around Chloe and leads her away as he continues to fill her head with images of stardom. "But, eh," he mutters quietly, "try to stay on the path from now on?"

Chloe winks at Cat and Egg as she is whisked away.

Mr. Spade adjusts his glasses and frowns at the four young sleuths. "You know," he says, "this seems more like tattling than detective work . . ."

"We know," Cat says. "We really thought Chloe had stolen the fruit."

"Or might have stolen the fruit," Egg adds.

Sam shrugs. "I didn't think it was her."

"Well," Mr. Spade says, patting Cat on the shoulder. "Next time you want to accuse a friend of stealing, be sure you're right, or you won't have that friend for very long."

THE END

TO FOLLOW ANOTHER PATH, TURN TO PAGE 11.

"Where were you when the mangosteen fruit was stolen," Sam barks, pointing suddenly at the tree, "from *that very tree* this morning?"

"I — " Chloe starts to say, staring at Sam. Suddenly, though, Chloe can say no more. She bursts into tears.

Sam and Gum jump up from the bench, sharing uneasy looks. Neither of them is good with criers.

Cat sits beside Chloe. "There, there," Cat says, putting a tentative arm around Chloe. "I know you feel bad. Everyone will forgive you for what you've done. It's hard feeling guilty."

Chloe barks, "I'm *not* guilty. I didn't steal anything! I'm crying because I can't believe anyone would think that about me!"

"I see," Cat says, looking at her friends with wide eyes. "And I completely understand."

"To think you four," Chloe says, "who I've been in school with since we were all in kindergarten, would think I would actually *steal*!"

Chloe shakes her head and wipes her eyes with the back of her hand. "And from a place like this," Chloe says. "A place I love, and have been coming to with my family since I was a baby!"

She looks at Cat. "Especially you, Cat," Chloe says. "I thought you and I were . . ."

"Friends?" Cat says.

Chloe's lip trembles and she nods slowly. "And you're also a vegetarian! You love animals too, right?"

"That's true," Cat says. "And I love the conservatory too. I was telling these three about how my dad used to take me here all the time during the winter."

"Mine too," Chloe says.

Cat's face brightens. "Maybe we were here at the same time when we were one year old!" she says.

Chloe laughs. "That would be funny," she says.

"All right, all right," Sam says, throwing up her hands. "So Chloe didn't do it."

TURN TO PAGE 85.

The alarm on Egg's phone rings. "Uh-oh," he says. "I guess we've been here a while. Time to get back to the lobby."

"The field trip's over already?" Cat says.

Gum glumly shoves his hands into his pocket and fetches a fresh piece of banana-watermelon gum. "Yup," he says. "Time to get back on the bus."

"And the case is still unsolved," Cat says.

"But we know two things," Chloe adds as she gets up.

She puts out her hand to help Cat up from the bench.

"What two things?" Cat asks.

Chloe smiles at her and says, "I didn't do it, and you didn't do it. And that's good enough for me."

"Three things," Cat says, smiling back at her. "We are definitely friends."

THE END

TO FOLLOW ANOTHER PATH, TURN TO PAGE 11.

"You sure know a lot about fruit!" Gum says as he and his three best friends stand in a half circle around Mr. Hill.

Mr. Hill's son, Wild Bill, sits on a bench nearby. But he sits with his head hanging backward off the front of the bench and his legs folded over the back.

"Yes," Mr. Hill says, moving toward another nearby tree. "Now, this tree here — "

"Even *I* know that one," Gum says. "That's a coconut tree."

"Incorrect," Mr. Hill says. "It is a papaya tree. The papaya is one of my favorites. It's a bit like a mango, but less tangy. The smell fills your sinuses as you eat. Delightful!"

"Wow," Sam says. "It's almost as if you've just eaten one!"

"Yes," Cat says. "You describe the taste so vividly!"

Mr. Hill waves off the kids' compliments as he strolls farther along the path.

As he passes the bench, Wild Bill rolls off and hops alongside his dad, occasionally running ahead in a circle and yelling "boo-bop!" for no earthly reason.

"That's why they call him Wild Bill," Egg says out of the corner of his mouth.

Cat snickers.

"How do you know so much about fruit, Mr. Hill?" Gum says when the chaperone glances at Egg and Cat.

"First of all," Mr. Hill says, leading the children into the next zone, "that was merely a papaya. Though a tropical fruit, it is common enough, available nowadays at most grocery stores."

Gum shrugs. "Maybe," he says, adding in a whisper to Sam beside him, "Actually I have a pack of papaya-mango in my pocket right now."

"Second of all," Mr. Hill goes on, his hands folded behind his back as he strolls along the brick path, "I happen to be a greengrocer by trade."

TURN THE PAGE.

"He doesn't look green," Gum says.

"It means he owns a fruit and vegetable store," Sam says. "I didn't know those existed anymore."

"It's tough," Mr. Hill says. "With the gigantic mega-supermarket on the edge of town, my little grocery on Old Main Street doesn't see the traffic it used to. But we get by."

Mr. Hill glances at his son. "Isn't that right, Bill?"

Wild Bill stops and thumps a fist against his chest. "We survive," he says.

With that, Wild Bill hurries along the path, disappearing around the bend.

"Now," Mr. Hill says, leaning down a little to look Gum and Sam right in the eye. "What's with the interrogation?"

"Um, interrogation?" Gum says.

"You think I don't know what you four busybodies are up to?" Mr. Hill says. "You think I've been snatching fruit off the conservatory's trees. I don't like the implication!"

TURN TO PAGE 96.

After a few moments, Sam leads her friends to the mangosteen tree.

"The scene of the crime," she says, crouching beside the little patch of soil.

"And Chloe came back," Cat says, "just like you always say, Sam: the crook always returns to the scene of the crime."

Sam hums thoughtfully as she scans the area.

Gum kneels beside her and reaches toward the dirt, but Sam grabs his wrist.

"Don't . . . touch . . . anything," Sam says.

"What's the big deal?" Cat asks.

"If we disturb the evidence," Sam explains, "we have no case."

Egg grins. "We still have my photo," he says, patting the camera around his neck. "That's all the evidence we need."

"Only if Chloe did it," Sam says.

"Oh, but she *must* have," Cat says, "even if she is a vegan."

TURN THE PAGE.

Carefully, Sam peers at the soil and the mangosteen tree's trunk. "Look there," Sam says, pointing at a patch of soil. "Those are Chloe's footprints."

"Sam," Egg says, holding up his camera, "we have photos of Chloe standing right there. We don't need the footprints."

"Yeah," Cat says. "This is a waste of time. If we take the photos to Mr. Spade, he'll know she's guilty."

"Guilty of crossing the barrier," Gum points out, "but not of stealing the fruit."

"She probably did, though," Cat says, crossing her arms and frowning.

Sam crawls along the barrier, still staring at the dark soil around the base of the mangosteen tree. Her sweaty T-shirt clings to her back.

"Couldn't someone have stolen an apple or something?" Sam says. "It's too hot in here."

"What exactly are you looking for?" Egg says, crouching beside her to look.

"I'll know it when I see . . ." she begins, and then her mouth turns up into a wide grin. "Aha! Look there!"

Sam points at a patch of soil, and the others see it at once, now that it's been pointed out.

"More footprints!" Cat says, shuffling up next to Sam. "And those aren't Chloe's, are they?"

Sam shakes her head. "Much too big," she says, rising to her feet. "Chloe might have stolen the fruit, but whoever's footprints these are is a likely suspect too."

"More likely to be the culprit," Gum points out, "since we know Chloe didn't steal anything while we watched her, and that's where the footprints probably came from."

Cat stands beside them.

"I don't think it was Chloe," Sam says. "We've been barking up the wrong tree."

"Okay," Gum says, "so what now? How do we track down whoever made these prints?"

TURN TO PAGE 99.

The four junior detectives jog through the tropics greenhouse and into the lobby.

"You don't think we should have talked to Chloe?" Egg asks Sam.

She shakes her head. "She seems suspicious," Sam says. "Especially since she told us she has fruit in her teeth."

"But?" Egg says.

"But, thinking more about it, she was with us when Cat found the rind of the mangosteen fruit," Sam says. "And she didn't act guilty."

Sam opens the door to the northern wing.

"Besides," Cat says, "we've known Chloe forever. I don't think she'd steal anything."

"There's Mr. Spade," Sam says as the four friends hurry along the path.

Mr. Spade is on the far side of a wooden bridge that crosses the little babbling brook.

"Mr. Spade!" Sam says, hurrying over the bridge. Then she spots the tour guide, standing right next to Mr. Spade, and she skids to a stop.

"Running is not permitted in the conservatory," the tour guide says.

Cat, Gum, and Egg jog up behind Sam.

"Oh," the guide says, glaring at Cat. "It's *you*."

"Hey," says Sam. "Cat didn't take *any* fruit, and we can prove it."

"Is that so?" the guide says, crossing his arms.

"Yes," Gum says. "Actually the person who stole the fruit is your volunteer!"

"Dan?" the guide says. "In the brown getup?"

"That's the guy," Sam says. "We even saw him eating it."

"Impossible," the guide says. "I saw your friend holding the mangosteen fruit's rind. How could you have seen him eating the same fruit?"

"Because I only found *half* of the rind," Cat says. "We saw him eat the other half."

The guide chews his cheek for a moment. "You know," he finally says, "I have wondered about Dan."

TURN THE PAGE.

"You have?" Mr. Spade says. "How so?"

The guide shrugs, as if it's no big deal. "He just gives me the creeps, you know?" he says. "Always has. And more than one visitor has said the same thing."

"We thought he was creepy too," Cat admits. "That's why we came to tell Mr. Spade, rather than confronting Dan ourselves."

The tour guide looks Cat right in the face and smiles. "Now, tell us," he says, "where did you see Dan?"

"Um," Cat says. "The second tropical greenhouse. He's probably still there. We got here pretty quick after we saw him."

"Right," the guide says, laughing. "Of course, I'll forgive the running in this case."

He glances at Mr. Spade. "To the South Pacific Greenhouse!"

Before long, the guide, Mr. Spade, and the four junior detectives step into the South Pacific Greenhouse.

"There he is!" Sam says immediately.

Turn to page 103.

"No, sir," Cat says, stepping between Mr. Hill and her friends. "Nothing of the kind. We're just . . . curious kids."

"By nature!" Egg adds.

Mr. Hill gives them a chilling glare and hurries after his son.

"Wait a minute," Sam says. "Let's let him think he's alone. Maybe we'll catch him in the act."

"Maybe he didn't do it," Cat says. "You heard him. It's a perfectly good explanation for why he knows so much about fruit."

"Maybe," Sam says. "But he seemed pretty defensive to me."

"How long do we wait?" Egg asks.

Sam taps her chin with the tip of her finger three times. "All right," she says. "Let's go. Stay out of sight and be quiet."

The four junior detectives move carefully along the path. Up ahead, Mr. Hill stops to read a marker.

Wild Bill runs laps around the edge of the koi pond in the center of the greenhouse.

Mr. Hill sits on a stone bench nearby and pulls off his backpack.

"Aha," Sam whispers. She and her friends push aside leaves and branches for a better glimpse. "This could be the moment we've been waiting for."

Mr. Hill unzips his backpack and reaches in. He pulls out a plastic baggy.

"I can't see what he's doing," Sam says.

"Hold on," Egg says, raising his camera. "I'll use the zoom on my camera."

But before he can switch on the display and zoom in, Wild Bill tumbles off the edge of the koi pond — right into the plants the four sleuths are hiding behind.

Mr. Hill jumps to his feet, shoving the baggy into his backpack as he does.

"Are you okay, Bill?" he calls.

Wild Bill looks up from the ground, dazed. "Hey," he says to the four friends looking down at him. "What are you guys doing?"

TURN THE PAGE.

Mr. Hill runs over to his son. He's surprised to see Cat, Egg, Gum, and Sam standing over Bill.

"What are you four up to now?" he asks. "Spying on me?"

"Oh, no," Cat says, her eyes wide. "It's nothing like that!"

But it's no use. Egg's camera is still in his hands, and Sam's notebook is in hers.

"Right," Mr. Hill says. "I'll see what Mr. Spade thinks about his students spying on adults from the bushes. Come on, Bill!"

With that, Mr. Hill and his son stride away.

"Uh-oh," Cat says. "We're in trouble."

Sam slumps against a tree trunk. "I guess we blew it," she says. "Another field trip we'll spend sitting on the bus with Smelly Mel."

Gum makes a face and holds his stomach. "I just hope he's not having liver and onions again!"

THE END

TO FOLLOW ANOTHER PATH, TURN TO PAGE 11.

"Shouldn't be too hard," Sam says. "We just need to get a photo of the prints and check everyone with big feet."

Egg steps up to the soil and raises his camera.

"Excuse me, kids," says a voice behind them.

The four sleuths flinch and step back.

The volunteer in the brown coveralls walks up to the mangosteen tree's barrier, wielding a wicked-looking steel-toothed bow rake.

"Looks like someone from your field trip broke the rules," he says, frowning. His expression is almost as frightening as the teeth of his rake. He obviously thinks they were the ones who crossed the barrier.

"It wasn't us!" Gum says.

The volunteer grunts and lowers the rake's teeth onto the ground. He pulls it across the dirt, leaving in its wake perfect lines in the soil.

In seconds, the footprints are gone.

Turn the page.

He faces them, the rake at his side like a sword. "Stay on the paths," he says, thumping the rake's handle on the bricks. "Don't make me tell you again!"

"But it wasn't us!" Cat insists.

The volunteer snarls at her and then stalks off, dragging the rake's handle along the path so the sound echoes through the greenhouse until he vanishes through the door to the next zone.

"He's grumpy," Gum says.

Sam nods. "I got a look at his shoes, too," she says. "Egg, let me have a look at the photos you took of the larger set of footprints."

"Photo?" Egg says. "Sam, I didn't *take* the photo. I didn't have a chance before that guy came along and raked them clean!"

Sam is too stunned to reply.

"But you had your camera out!" Gum says. "You just had to push a button!"

TURN TO PAGE 102.

"I didn't know he was about to rake out the footprints. Why would he do that?" Egg says.

Sam narrows her eyes. "To hide the evidence," she says, her voice cold. "To cover his tracks."

"Literally," Gum says.

"So he's won," Sam says, squinting toward the door the volunteer left through, "this time."

"Um, Sam?" Egg says. He holds out his wrist to show her the time. "The field trip is over in half an hour. There's no 'this time.' We'll never see that guy again."

"We're out of chances," Cat says.

"We blew it," Gum says.

"And Mr. Spade and the conservatory guide still think *I* stole that fruit," Cat says. She drops onto a bench and puts her chin in her hands.

Sam sits beside her. "I'm sorry, Cat," she says. "We've been beaten by a criminal mastermind."

THE END

TO FOLLOW ANOTHER PATH, TURN TO PAGE 11.

Dan the volunteer still sits on the edge of the pond where they last saw him. Also nearby are Mr. Hill, Wild Bill, Anton, and Anton's goon friends, Hans and Luca.

"But he doesn't have any fruit," Cat points out.

The four friends lead the way along the path right up to Dan. He holds a napkin to his mouth and smiles.

"Dan," the tour guide says. "Have you been snacking?"

Dan nods. "Just finished a pear," he says. "Juicy and sweet. Perfect pear. Couldn't be happier with it."

"Of course not," says Mr. Hill, stepping up to the group gathered around the volunteer. "Because you bought it at my store on Old Main Street, isn't that right?"

"Just a minute," the tour guide says. "Are you telling me you just ate a pear, not the stolen mangosteen fruit?"

The volunteer gives the tour guide an icy stare for a moment.

TURN THE PAGE.

"I can't prove I ate a pear," Dan says. "And you can't prove I ate the mangosteen. So I guess we'll never know the truth."

Suddenly, Sam steps up and shouts, "Aha!"

Everyone turns and looks at her.

"Egg," she says, keeping her eyes fixed on Dan the volunteer, "show us the photos of the crime scene you took a few minutes ago."

"Okay," Egg says, clicking on his camera. He scrolls through, showing Sam the display as he goes.

"Stop!" Sam says. "Zoom in on that one. A little to the right. There!"

"It's a footprint," Egg says.

"Let me see that," the tour guide says, looking over Sam's and Egg's shoulders. "Ah!"

The tour guide runs over to Dan the volunteer and snatches the shoe right off his foot. "Now we'll see!" he announces, running back to Egg and his camera.

The tour guide holds the shoe upside down

right next to the little display. His eyes dart back and forth between the screen and the tread. Finally, he frowns.

"They don't match," he says. "Dan didn't do it." He tosses the shoe back to Dan.

Sam's face falls. "But I was so sure!" she says.

Cat pats Sam on the back to comfort her, but just then the tour guide spins on her.

"And as for you!" he snaps at Cat. "After your friends' sloppy attempt to meddle, I'm even more convinced of your guilt!"

He turns to Mr. Spade. "Sir," the tour guide says, "please put these four students on the bus until your field trip is over." With that, the tour guide walks off.

Mr. Spade sighs. "You heard him, kids."

"Great," Gum says. "Back on the bus to be bored. I sure hope Smelly Mel is finished with his lunch by now."

THE END

TO FOLLOW ANOTHER PATH, TURN TO PAGE 11.

literary news

MYSTERIOUS WRITER REVEALED!

Steve Brezenoff is the author of the Field Trip Mysteries, the Museum Mysteries, and the Ravens Pass series of thrillers, as well as three novels for older readers. Steve lives in Minneapolis, Minnesota, with his wife, Beth, and their two children, Sam and Etta.

arts & entertainment

ARTIST IS KEY TO SOLVING MYSTERY, SAY POLICE

Marcos Calo lives happily in A Coruña, Spain, with his wife, Patricia (who is also an illustrator), and their daughter, Claudia. When Marcos and Patricia aren't drawing, they like to go on long walks by the sea. They also watch a lot of films and eat Nutella sandwiches. Yum!

A Detective's Dictionary

atrium – an area in a building that is open and has windows to allow light in

fork (in a path) – a path that splits in two

greengrocer – a person who sells fruits and vegetables

greenhouse – a building or section of a building made of windows that is used to grow plants

henchman – the sidekick of a powerful person; one who does someone else's dirty work for them

hinky – causing suspicion

implication – a suggestion that isn't said directly

nostalgic – a feeling of missing something or someone

parka – a winter coat

snicker – to laugh in a short, quiet way

vandal – someone who destroys property

vivid – bright or full of details

FURTHER INVESTIGATIONS

CASE #YCSFTMTMBS17

1. The four detectives sometimes jump to conclusions and accuse people of stealing the fruit. Do you think this causes problems? Can you think of a time in the story when this hurt someone's feelings?

2. Who were the suspects in the case of the disappearing fruit? What clues in the text made them seem suspicious?

3. Cat was accused of eating the mangosteen fruit when she hadn't. Have you ever been accused of something you didn't do? What did that feel like?

IN YOUR OWN DETECTIVE'S NOTEBOOK . . .

1. Write a letter from Mr. Hill to the conservatory apologizing for stealing the mangosteen fruit. What reasons do you think he would give for taking the seeds?

2. The four sleuths really dislike spending time on the bus with Smelly Mel. Can you list reasons that Smelly Mel may not want to be on the bus with Sam, Egg, Cat, and Gum?

3. Chloe steps over a guide rope to take a closer look at a tree for her drawing. Write down three reasons this might not be a good idea.

Ready to choose your next MYSTERY?

Check out all the books in the
You Choose Stories Field Trip Mysteries!

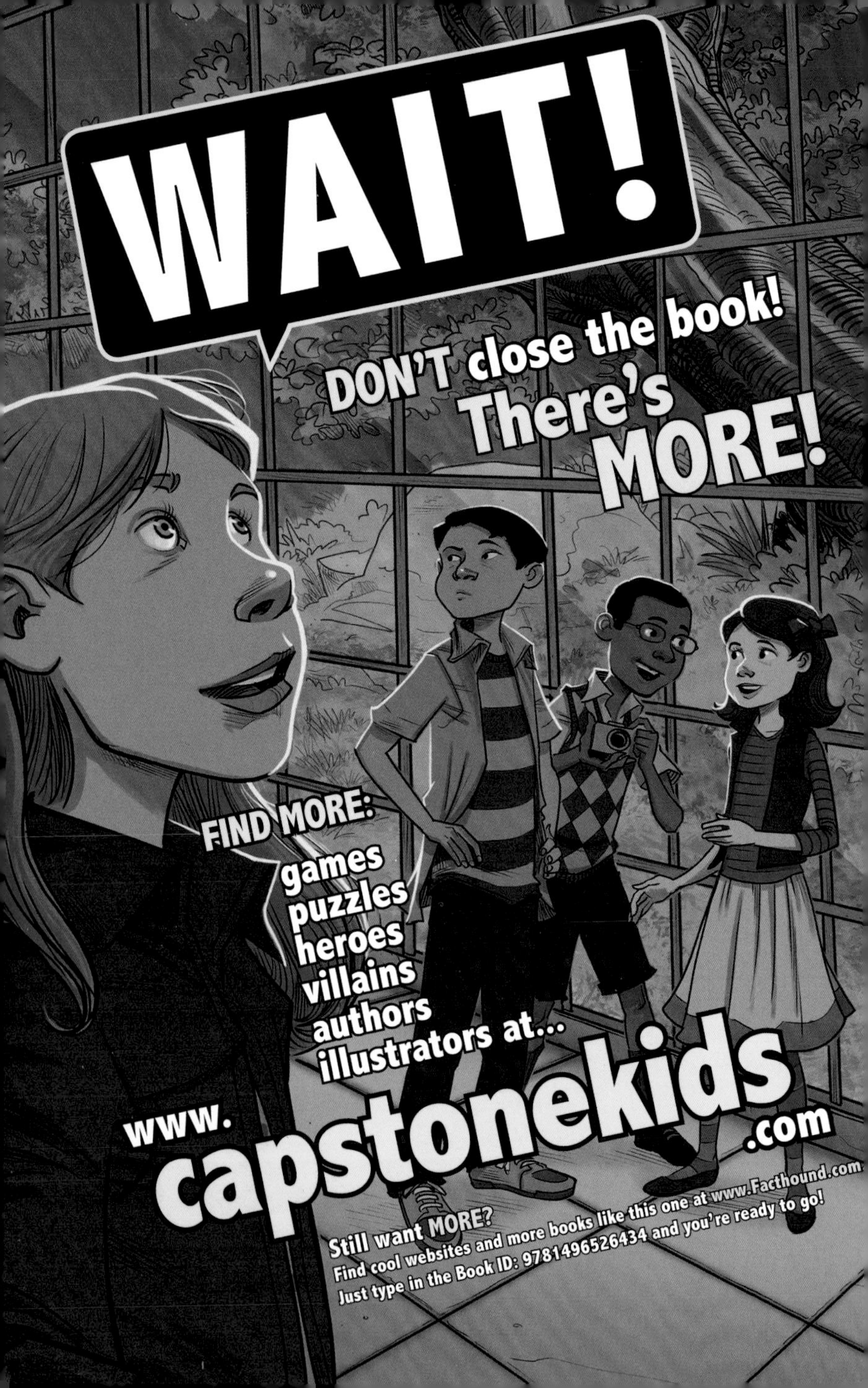
WAIT!
DON'T close the book!
There's MORE!
FIND MORE:
games
puzzles
heroes
villains
authors
illustrators at...
www.capstonekids.com
Still want MORE?
Find cool websites and more books like this one at www.Facthound.com.
Just type in the Book ID: 9781496526434 and you're ready to go!